# *Love Letters and Other Stories*

**SCHOLASTIC INC.**
New York  Toronto  London  Auckland  Sydney
Mexico City  New Delhi  Hong Kong

# Love Letters and Other Stories

### Short stories by

**Michelle Calero**
**Kate Walker**
**Jane Yolen**
**Heidi Elisabet Yolen Stemple**
**Gloria D. Miklowitz**
**Norma Fox Mazer**

**SCHOLASTIC INC.**
New York  Toronto  London  Auckland  Sydney
Mexico City  New Delhi  Hong Kong

## Cover illustration by
## Luc Latulippe

## Illustrations by
## Shawn Banner

# Contents

# I Thought You Loved Me

Michelle Calero

On her way home from school, Carmen decided to stop by the *bodega* and get something to drink. "What are you going to get, Carmen?" asked her friend Dora.

"Maybe a Coke, even though Mami hates it when I drink it. Some sob story about it being bad for you. Big deal. If that was true, every teenager on this earth would be in the hospital. I don't care. One little can of soda never hurt anyone."

The two girls went into the corner grocery store, and they each bought a can of soda. Then Carmen saw him standing there—the new kid on the block who went by the name of Chico. He had just come from Puerto Rico, and it showed. Brown skin tone, dark brown hair, deep brown eyes. He was perfect—perfect in every way. He was smart (they were in the same class), he was extremely good looking, and she knew he was nice, even though the only words he ever spoke to her were, "Excuse me."

Carmen had to talk with him. She just had to. So Carmen told Dora, "Go on ahead, I have to buy something else."

"Don't worry, Carmen, I can take a hint." Dora walked out, acting like a true best friend. Carmen walked over to the rack where the snack-sized cakes were and carefully selected something that cost more money than she had in her pocket. When the clerk announced to her, loud enough for Chico to hear, that the cake cost fifty cents, Carmen **magnanimously** said that she only had forty cents.

"I got it," said Chico, and placed a shiny silver dime on the counter.

"Thank you," she said, and gave him a piece of the cake.

"Don't mention it. So where are you headed?"

"Home," she said. She couldn't believe she was actually talking to him.

"And where is your home?"

"About five blocks away, on Mango Street."

"If you want, I can walk you home. I only live two blocks from Mango Street, so it's not really out of my way."

Carmen thought she had died and gone to heaven.

"Sure."

The two teenagers began walking, and about five minutes later, Carmen found her hand holding his. She only wished the walk had been longer.

Monday morning Carmen told Dora what had happened that day at the store. "I'm sorry I couldn't call to tell you sooner, but I had to go shopping with my mother."

"That's okay."

As the girls were walking down the school **corridor**, they saw Chico heading in their direction. He just passed Carmen by. She was shocked. She couldn't believe that after what happened on Friday he would act cold and not even give her as much as a glance or a hello.

During lunch outside, Carmen tried to get his attention. She called to him. "Hi, Chico!"

"What? Oh, yeah. Hi, uh, Carmen."

"Thanks again about Friday."

There was no response. When Carmen looked up from examining her sneakers, he was gone. Once again she was shrugged off by Chico. What was going on?

Carmen called Dora and asked her what she should do about Chico. She knew she could count on Dora to listen and give her the right advice. "I don't know what to do, Dora," she **confided**. "After what happened in the store and everything, I thought. . ."

"Carmen, I'm going to tell you something that I think will make you happy." Carmen expected to hear something good about Dora's family. She never expected what she was about to learn. "About a week ago, I asked Chico if he liked you. He said he would tell me at lunch. I don't know what happened, but he never told me."

"Yeah? Go on."

"Well, the next day he came up to me at lunch, and he said he did like you. Then I asked him if he wanted me to tell you, and he said 'No, that's okay, I'll do it myself.'"

"But then how come he's been ignoring me?" Carmen asked.

After weeks of constantly being ignored, Carmen soon got tired of running home and crying. No more tears could fall from her eyes. Then she came to a decision. She would confront him, one-on-one—no friends, no notes. It was now or never. This was just something she had to do.

She planned everything very carefully, what she would say and when she would say it. She decided that the best time was at lunch, when they could walk around and settle things. Between classes was not a good time because too many people would be crowded in the halls, and everyone was usually in a hurry. Yes, lunch was the best time. They would have

plenty of time to talk, and the **atmosphere** would be relaxed.

The next day, after the lunch bell rang, Carmen felt a tightening in her stomach. She ignored it. There was only one week until graduation and again, it was now or never. She waited by the cafeteria door. Chico passed by, and of course she was brushed off. She quickly ate her lunch and waited until he was done to catch him walking through the door into the yard.

"Chico, come here."

Chico slowly walked up to her and said, "Yeah?"

"Look, there's something I've been wanting to tell you and I. . . ."

"Look, I'm sorry I've been ignoring you," Chico said. "I just had to think things over, and I've made up my mind. Would you go out with me?"

Carmen couldn't believe what she was hearing. She had been waiting for this moment all year.

"I'm sorry, Chico. I only think of you as a friend and nothing more." Chico walked away with a sad look of disappointment on his face.

# Love Letters

Kate Walker

My name's Nick, and my girlfriend's name is Fleur, and she has a friend called Helen who's got a boyfriend named Clive. Now this Clive is really weird, or at least, he does one weird thing I know of—he writes three-page letters to his girlfriend, Helen, *every* day.

"What's wrong with the nerd?" I asked Fleur, after she'd spent a whole lunchtime telling me about him.

"There's nothing *wrong* with him," she said. "You're so unromantic, Nick."

"Of course I'm not unromantic," I said, but when I offered her a lick of my ice cream to prove it, she groaned, pulled her gym bag over her head, and refused to talk to me anymore.

When girls go quiet, that's a bad sign.

"What's wrong?" I asked her.

"You don't love me," she said.

"Of course I do," I assured her, offering her my entire ice cream. She wouldn't take it.

"You don't love me *enough*," she said.

"How much is *enough*?" I replied. *How much ice cream did it take?* I thought.

"You don't write *me* letters like Clive does to Helen," she said.

"I don't need to write you letters—I see you every day in computer class," I said, "*and* chemistry."

"Clive sees Helen every day in biology, math, and homeroom," she said, "and he writes letters to *her*!"

I knew what was happening here—my girlfriend was cooling on me, and pretty soon she'd be ready to dump me altogether.

"Okay," I said, "I'll write you a letter."

"Aw, Nick," she cried, whipping her gym bag off her head.

I was glad I'd weakened because Fleur is really gorgeous, and I couldn't risk losing her over a few lines scrawled on a piece of paper.

I sat down that night and began my first letter: "Dear Fleur...." Then I stared at the page for the next half-hour. What do you write to someone you see every day? I **gnawed** my pencil, I chewed my nails, and then, in **desperation**, I finally asked Mom.

"Write about things you have in common," Mom suggested, so I wrote the following: "Wasn't that computer class on Tuesday hilarious? The best part was when Brando tilted the computer to show us the little button underneath and the monitor crashed to the floor."

I wrote about our chemistry class, too, though it wasn't quite as interesting because not a single kid messed up their experiment.

The next day, I got the letter back with a "D-" marked on the bottom.

"What was wrong with it?" I asked Fleur.

"You made a lot of spelling mistakes, for one thing," she said.

"I was being *myself*," I told her.

"I didn't really notice," she said. "I mean,

you didn't say anything personal in it at all!"
Is that what she wanted, a *personal* letter?
I **pondered** this for a few minutes. There
were guys all around the cafeteria just waiting
to take my place and share their chocolate milk
with the fabulous Fleur. If revealing a few
personal secrets was what it took to hang on
to her, I could manage that.

"Dear Fleur," I began the second letter that
night, "This is not something I'd reveal to just
anyone, but I use underarm deodorant—only
on gym day or in really hot weather, of course."

No, scratch that—that was *too* personal. I
ripped up the page and started again. "Dear
Fleur, You'll never believe what happened to
me today. Mrs. Hessel blew up at me in history
class for absolutely no reason. I was completely
**mortified**, and Goggle-eyes Gilda laughed her
stupid head off."

Actually, once I started, I found the
personal stuff not that hard to write. I told
Fleur what grade I really got on the English
midterm. Then I told her about a movie I'd
seen where this pioneer guy loses his plow

horse, then he loses his wife, then he loses his children, and then his cows get hoof rot. But even though he sits down and bawls his eyes out about it, in the end he walks off into the sunset, a stronger man.

"I'd like to suffer a great personal loss like that," I confessed to Fleur in the letter, "and walk away stronger and **nobler** for it."

Her sole comment on letter number two was, "You didn't say anything in it about *me*." Then she deserted me to eat lunch with Helen.

It was time to hit the panic button—Fleur was drifting away from me. I stuffed my sandwiches back in my bag and went looking for Clive, cornering him under the stairwell.

"Okay, Clive, what are all these wonderfully romantic things you write in your letters to Helen?" I asked.

Clive turned out to be a decent kid—he not only told me what he wrote, he gave me a photocopy of the latest letter he was writing to Helen.

You should have seen it!

"Darling Helen, Your hair is like spun gold,

and your eyes remind me of twilight reflected on Throsby Creek. Your ear lobes are... Your eyelashes are..." It was what you'd call a poetic **autopsy**.

And as if that weren't syrupy enough, he then continued on to the **declarations** of love: "You're precious to me because blah, blah, blah. I yearn for you in history class because blah, blah, blah. I can't eat noodles without thinking of you because blah, blah, blah."

"Do girls really go for this mushy sort of thing?" I asked him.

"Helen thinks it's fantastic," he said. "She'd drop me tomorrow if I stopped writing her letters. It's the price you pay if you want to keep your girlfriend."

So I began my third letter, with Clive's photocopy propped up in front of me as a guide.

"Dear Fleur, Your hair is like..." I began.

Actually, I'd always thought it was pretty from a distance but gooey when you touched it—too much gel, maybe.

I scrapped that opening and started again.

"Dear Fleur, Your eyes are like..."

Actually, they're a bit small and squinty—I think she might need glasses.

Forget about her eyes.

"Dear Fleur, Your face is excellent overall. You look like one of those soap opera actresses."

I thought I would have been able to go on for hours about her face, but having commented on its general excellence, that seemed to sum things up.

I moved on to the declarations: "I love you

because...." Once again I gnawed my pencil and chewed my fingernails—but this time I couldn't ask Mom.

Why *did* I love Fleur, I wondered. Because she was spunky? Because all the other guys thought so, too? Well, not all of them—some of them thought she wasn't all that interesting to talk to, but I **attributed** that to jealousy.

Still, I began to wonder, what *had* we talked about in the three weeks we'd been going out? There wasn't much to our conversations, really. She'd never been interested enough in my hockey playing to ask in-depth questions about it, and, I have to admit, I hadn't found her description of her new ankle boots all that **riveting** either.

No wonder I was having so much trouble writing letters to her—we had nothing in common. I barely knew her. What were her views on nuclear waste disposal? Was she for or against capital punishment?

I scrapped the letter, scrapped Clive's photocopy, and started again, only this time the words flowed with no trouble at all.

"Dear Fleur, This writing of letters was an excellent idea because it gives me the opportunity to say something very important to you. I think you're a nice girl, and I've enjoyed going out with you for three weeks, but I think we should call it quits. Even if it's a great personal loss to both of us, I know we'll walk away stronger and nobler as a result. Yours sincerely, Nick."

I slipped the letter to her in computer class. She didn't seem too **devastated** by it—she just ripped it up without saying a word. But then, two days later, photocopies of my second letter, the really personal one, began **circulating** around school.

I didn't mind, though, because as a result of that, Goggle-eyes Gilda slipped me a note in history that said, briefly, "I like your style, Nick. You've got depth." I took another look at Goggle-eyes and realized I didn't mind her style either—she has this terrific laugh, and she's a whiz on computers.

I responded right away, but this time I wrote my own kind of letter—honest and to the point, without any advice from my mother or Clive. "Dear Gilda, That three-minute talk you gave on speech day about Third World **famine** relief was fascinating. I'll be eating lunch at noon today if you'd care to join me in the school cafeteria."

# Opening Act

Jane Yolen and Heidi Elisabet Yolen Stemple

She's not exactly famous—more like well known. At least if you live in our county you'd know her name, and chances are you'd have heard her perform at a church or at somebody's wedding.

She won the grand prize on a show like *Star Search* about ten years ago, before there even was a *Star Search*—back when I was small enough to think that was a big deal. Daddy videotaped the show, and I must have watched the tape a hundred times, but to tell the truth, it's real embarrassing now—her cheesy songs about love gone wrong and how another guy dumped her.

Once I asked her how she'd even know what being dumped felt like when she's been married to Daddy for about a million years. I mean, sometimes they still act like teenagers. She just laughed and said it was a feeling no one ever forgets, even if it was a million years ago.

Ever since I can remember, everyone has always asked me if I want to be a singer like my mom when I grow up. It's understandable, I suppose—Mom used to take me onstage with her when I was little. I guess it was cute when I was three and four and five years old, but when it got painful—for both the audience and me—she stopped. One day I was the star of the family, the next day I was nothing, and I didn't understand, really, till I turned twelve and was kicked out of the school choir. It seems I can't carry a tune—not even in a bucket loader.

I guess I **inherited** my dad's genes when it comes to music—he left Woodstock and became an accountant. Anyway, these days I can't even imagine how terrifying it must be to get up and perform in front of an audience. I think I'd rather be an accountant like Dad, not that anyone ever asks me about that.

On the other hand, my older brother, Aaron, is a bigger ham than Mom. He has his own band in Minneapolis, and he sings, plays the guitar, and even writes his own music. He's the real star—Mom walks around the house humming his tunes, and my dad, Mr. "I only listen to country music," **abandoned** his Willie Nelson CDs in favor of Aaron's latest album. Sometimes I even catch myself singing his songs—with my voice!

Maybe I can't sing, but I do understand the kind of heartbreak described in my mom's songs—which brings me to my reason for telling this story. Right after school started this fall, I heard from a "friend" that my boyfriend, Jeff, had been eyeing Marie McCall.

Now, I had never liked the way he looked at her in the school hallways between classes, but a lot of boys looked at Marie that way, especially now that she—unlike me—had grown quite a bit over summer vacation. And since Jeff hadn't called me since school started, I suspected that meant we were breaking up after a whole summer together, though I hoped I was wrong.

However, the last thing I would have done was get up onstage and sing about it. *As summer slipped into the fall, you dumped me for Marie McCall*—what a catchy tune.

I've always thought the best way to deal with heartbreak is to write poetry in secret— like the 27 poems I wrote about Brian, my last boyfriend, who moved to Texas when his mom was offered a great job there. It's better than wailing about fake heartbreak on a stage, anyway. I keep my poems safely tucked away in a box in the back of my closet. After all, they're no one's business but my own.

When the phone rang last week at 10:30, I jumped to answer it. I was up late studying for my advanced math test, and my parents were watching TV. I knew, in that way you just know, that the phone was for me. Sure enough, it was my best friend, Kaytlin. She had been at the mall, not needing to study because she isn't in an advanced anything class.

"Manda," she said, out of breath, "this

couldn't wait till morning—it's too important."
There was an edge to her voice that I couldn't
quite grasp. "Are you ready? Are you sitting
down?"

"Yes," I said, although I wasn't.

"Manda, it's Jeff—I saw him with Marie
McCall." That's when I sat down. "They were
coming out of the movies together, and I
followed them."

Although there was nothing amusing
about this, I almost smiled—Kaytlin wants to
be a police officer like her father and three
older brothers, and she tends to act as if she
were already undercover.

"Were you **lurking**?" I asked.

I could just see her pulling her jacket up
around her face and sneaking about.
Sometimes I'm jealous that she knows exactly
what she wants to be.

"After about half an hour of
**surveillance**—are you sure you're sitting?"

I made an **affirmative** sound.

"He kissed her."

Suddenly I didn't want any details. "Kate,

I've got to go—my mom's calling me," I lied. I'm sure she knew I wasn't telling the truth.

I abandoned my books and ran upstairs. I hate crying, really, but it seemed like the appropriate thing to do—so I did, into my pillow, where no one could hear me.

After I'd cried as much as I could, I started writing in my poetry journal. I was inspired—heartbreak does that to me—and the rhymes had nothing to do with Marie or McCall or Jeff. They had to do with me and with poetry.

*I'm picking up the pieces of my heart.*
*First you mended it, then tore it all apart.*
*You've made despair an art form*
*And cheating an art.*

I was feeling better in a strange sort of way. I'd read somewhere that many poets find poetry a **catharsis**. I could definitely understand that, so I continued:

*You tore down my palace and my throne,*
*The ones I'd built of **mortar** and of bone.*
*You **razed** it piece by piece,*
*Each precious little stone.*

I loved that word *razed.*

I wrote for another hour or so, crossing lines out, rewriting the rhymes. It always happens that way—the first **stanza** or two come quickly, but the following ones need to be worked and reworked. As I wrote, the writing itself became my entire universe, rhyme and **meter** replacing tears and pain.

When I was done, I reread the whole poem aloud. I was happy with it—and exhausted.

I must have fallen asleep, because the next moment it was morning and I was still in my clothes. But, curiously, someone had tucked me neatly under the covers, and the lights were off.

My journal, however, was nowhere to be found. Worrying about my math test and wondering what could have happened to my journal, I went downstairs to breakfast.

When I got there, my dad was reading the financial section of the paper, as usual, and Mom was sipping her tea. It seemed normal enough, until I spotted my poetry notebook next to her bread plate, covered with crumbs from her toast.

I snatched up the notebook and shrieked— for all I knew, they'd been having a good laugh at my expense over their breakfast of cereal and toast.

"Manda, honey," Mom began, "these are—"

I cut her off, too mad to hear her excuses— or, worse, her **criticisms** of my work. "You had no right to **violate** my privacy," I squeaked. I always squeak when I'm really angry, which sort of **undercuts** the effect. Turning, I stomped out, slamming the door behind me like one enormous exclamation

point. I was halfway to school before I realized I had left without my books or jacket, and to make matters worse, I was early for school.

My anger brewed through first-period social studies, my stomach growled through the second-period math test, and by the time I reached lunch, I had decided that not speaking to my mother was the only way to deal with her. She might *read* my words, but I sure wasn't going to let her *hear* them. I was so mad that I forgot to be heartbroken, till I saw Jeff walking hand in hand with Marie McCall.

"I don't know who I hate more," I told Kaytlin.

"What do you mean?" she asked.

"My mom or Jeff—they both broke faith with me," I explained.

"I thought Jeff broke your heart," she said.

"Whatever."

I didn't want to talk to Kaytlin anymore—she just didn't get it. I really wanted to call my brother, Aaron, but he was on tour with his band. However, since they were headed our way for a Friday night gig at the Iron Horse Cafe, three days away, I supposed I could wait until after the show. I might not want to talk to Mom, and I couldn't talk to Kaytlin, but Aaron was going to get an earful!

The three long days until Friday seemed closer to a year and a half, but somehow I made it through.

Mom tried several times to talk to me. Once in the kitchen, she stopped me in the middle of making a peanut butter sandwich and said, "Manda, your poem is..." And once at the dinner table she began, "Honey, you've got to let me..." But I walked out each time, letting the door slams be double exclamation points. She finally got the message and left me alone. Just maybe, I thought, she knew she was wrong. Just maybe, I thought, I'd stop being mad a year from now.

Even Dad tried to get into the act, saying, "Your mom thought the notebook was homework, Manda. It's a terrific poem and..."

And I cut him off too, saying, "She sings about broken hearts, but I live them. I don't want to talk about it." So we didn't.

To make things easier, Mom had nightly rehearsals with her group, as they were the opening act for Aaron's band, so every night when she got home, I was already in bed, pretending to sleep.

And then—suddenly—it was Friday. I was so excited to see my brother, I didn't mind having to listen to Mom's group first. She had already left for her sound check, so Daddy and I drove over together, talking about everything: the new pizza parlor in town, my math test, my brother's band. Everything, in fact, except my fight with Mom—Daddy was too **diplomatic** to bring that up again. It came from dealing with crazed clients at tax season, I guess.

At the Iron Horse, we were given the best table in the house and treated like the family of royalty, which, on this night, I guess we were. The owner of the club, Mom's self-professed "biggest fan," came to our table twice to make sure we were comfortable.

Finally, the lights dimmed, and it was time for Mom to take the stage. At other times, I had found this a magic moment, the lights going down, her name called over the speakers, the applause, and then her entrance. But I was still too mad at her to let the magic work, and for the first time it all seemed a little—I don't know—**tawdry**, maybe?

She started her set with a **raucous** jazzy number that got the entire audience clapping in time with the beat. I didn't clap on principle—after all, she was still the woman who had stolen my journal and read my most secret poetry. Still, I had to admit, she looked wonderful in her white gauzy dress, and she sounded great, too, so maybe a little bit of the magic still worked. I couldn't help tapping my foot to the beat of the music, but when I realized what I was doing, I made myself stop.

Then she pulled up a stool and sat for a soulful **ballad** that cried out for a lost boyfriend, long gone, but not forgotten. As usual, it made me blush—but even more than that, it made me think about Jeff and how he had left me for Marie McCall. I let the lyrics wash over me, tell me my own story, and—you know—I felt better. Other people had suffered before, and it wasn't the end of the world. Maybe that's what music does best—reminds us that we are like other people.

Mom sang three more songs and then finished with an old lullaby—one she used to sing to me as a kid whenever I was sick or scared of the dark. This time she sang it with a slight blues beat and it seemed—somehow—like a kind of apology. Then she blew kisses to the audience, acknowledged her band, bowed, and turned to go.

This was a **ploy** I had seen many times before—she wasn't ready to leave yet, and she knew the audience would yell for just one more song. Even though I knew it was a practiced routine, she seemed believable when she turned and slowly walked back to the microphone.

"As many of you know," Mom started, her voice low and **husky**, "tonight is a very special night for me. My son's band is patiently awaiting our departure from the stage so they can come out and show you their stuff."

I could feel the excitement building and had to admire the way she controlled the audience. Even I was energized.

"But what you don't know—and I wasn't even fully aware of until this very week—is that he isn't my only talented child."

I heard my mother's words but didn't quite get it. Call me slow, but I was waiting for Aaron to come on.

"Amanda, honey, could you join me

onstage?" I heard my name, and suddenly there was a spotlight on me, and my dad was pulling me to my feet. As if in a **haze**, I stood and looked at my mother, who was motioning to me. My anger at her for embarrassing me in front of all these people was small compared to my overwhelming fear. I hadn't been up onstage in ten years. She couldn't possibly mean for me to go up there and—do what—*sing*, with my voice?

Then Daddy gave me a push from behind and my feet seemed to move on their own as I walked, shaking all the way, onto the stage.

Mom hugged me, though I was **rigid** with anger and fear. I smiled a weak smile and attempted a **feeble** escape, but she led me to the empty stool, where she sat me down. Then she began talking again. I only made out parts of what she was saying.

"... which she wrote... doesn't know... hope you like it as much as..."

And as I sat, red-faced and shaking, her backup group started to play a slow, sad melody.

When she sang the opening lines, I could

hardly believe it.

*I'm picking up the pieces of my heart; first you mended it, and then tore it apart. You've made despair an art form, and cheating an art. I'm picking up the pieces of my heart.*

After the first stanza, she looked at me and smiled. My face must have **registered** shock and horror, because she moved closer while the band played an instrumental section. Then she picked up my limp right hand, and her eyes told me to look out into the crowd. I looked—it was better than staring at her—but I could only see a couple of rows into the darkened café.

*You tore down my palace and my throne...*

As she started singing again, my dad's face was the first I focused on. He had an awfully odd expression. I couldn't tell if there was a kind of feedback from the spotlight, but he almost seemed to have tears in his eyes. I may have started to smile.

*The ones I'd built of mortar and of bone.*

I looked past him to strangers in the audience and saw that they were swaying to the music. Now I knew I was smiling.

*You took it down slow, piece by piece—each precious little stone.*

I looked just offstage to my right. Aaron and the guys in his band were all watching and listening—and grinning. I grinned back. I just couldn't help it.

*You tore down my palace and my throne.*

Mom squeezed my hand, and I closed my eyes while she finished the song—our song.

When the music ended, I opened my eyes again. Everyone was clapping and cheering. One by one, they began to stand. Mom released my hand and took a bow. Then she turned to me and pulled me up by the shoulders to stand beside her.

"*Razed*," I whispered. "*Razed* it piece by piece. You changed my words. How could you?"

"Words on a page," she whispered back, "are not the same as words in the mouth. Trust me on this one, sweetie. Now bow—the applause is for you."

I looked for my brother, but he had disappeared. Only his band remained, applauding along with the crowd. Suddenly I realized what Mom had said—I was supposed to bow. I tried, but have you ever bowed when your knees are shaking with anger—and with joy? All I managed was some sort of bob.

Then the audience began roaring even louder, so I bowed again—this time a deep one—and when I came up from my bow, Aaron was there with a bouquet of red roses. He handed them to me and kissed my cheek.

"So," he said, "you've been holding out on me, Sis, letting me struggle with my own lousy lyrics. Are you going to write something for me, too?"

"You don't sing about heartbreak," I said. "No one has ever dumped you."

"I sing about lots of things that have never happened to me," he said.

"What about *razing*?" I asked.

He laughed. He didn't know what I was talking about, but it didn't matter. "Up or down?" he asked. Then he laughed again. "Now get off the stage—it's my turn now."

As I sat next to Daddy, I thought, *You raised me up, I razed you down....* It was the start of a song, and Aaron could sing it—or Mom. Whatever.

# My Side of the Story

Gloria D. Miklowitz

**Cassie**

"Cass, how nice to see you again," Janet, Dad's new wife, says as she opens the door. She's wearing old jeans and an oversized shirt, and she has a mostly bald baby in her arms. Her son, Paul, stands beside her with a superior smirk on his face.

Dad had remarried and moved out of state, so I only saw him when he came to Los Angeles on business—until now. Now he's moved back and bought a house for his new family, and he wants me to visit every other weekend.

"Come in, come in, Cass," Janet says, holding the baby like a shield, the same way I'm holding my tennis racket and stuffed animal Eeyore. "Paul, take Cass's bag to the

baby's room. James, honey, Cass is here!"

Dad storms into the room, holding a big packing box. He sets it down and spreads his arms wide. "Cass, sweetheart—come here and give your old dad a hug!"

He's the same dad, with the same happy grin for me, but with them around, it's not the same. I let Dad embrace me, the donkey and the racket caught between us.

"My goodness," he exclaims, drawing back, "you haven't met the most important member of our family yet—your baby sister!"

Janet turns to give me a better view of Sabina, whose head is **nestled** on Janet's shoulder. The baby has big hazel eyes, like Dad's, a pretty mouth, and rosy cheeks.

"Do you want to hold her?" Janet asks.

I know what Janet's trying to do, and I won't let her win me over. "No thanks. I'd like to go to my room now, please."

"Sure, honey," Dad says, "just follow Paul, and as soon as you're settled, come out to the back and we'll have a cool drink together."

I hear their low voices as I follow Paul to

the baby's room, and I have to wonder if they're talking about me. Paul opens the door to a small room with a crib and a single bed. "Sabina doesn't cry anymore at night, so she shouldn't wake you," he assures me, tossing my bag onto the bed. Then he gazes at me with a silly grin that puts me on guard and says, "Tell me, the way you hold onto that stuffed animal makes me wonder—is it part of you?"

Stunned, I open my mouth, then close it. "That's my father's jogging suit you're wearing," I shout with as much meanness as I feel. "I gave it to him for Christmas!"

"Here, then," he cries, as he starts to peel off the top. His goofy smile is gone now.

"Get out of here," I scream, dropping Eeyore and pushing Paul out the door. "I hate you! I hate all of you! I didn't even want to come here!" I slam the door and throw myself on the bed. I can't believe I'm going to spend a whole weekend with strangers! I came to see Dad, not Janet or Paul or that bald baby!

"Cassie, sweetheart," Dad says gently, knocking on the door, "we're waiting for you.

Janet's baked some chocolate nut cookies just for you." When I don't answer, he calls out, "Here I come, ready or not," and opens the door. He sits down on the bed, but I turn away.

"I know it's hard for you, honey," he says, "but give us a chance. Maybe when we get better settled, you and I can play tennis, take a walk or something, okay? Now come outside and join the fun."

They look so cozy, sitting around the picnic table, Janet's face upturned for Dad's kiss and Paul holding the baby, who's chewing on a set of plastic keys. When she sees me, she says, "Ah ga!"

"She likes you," Janet exclaims, passing me a glass of juice.

"Aren't Janet's cookies fabulous?" Dad asks.

I nod to please him.

"Remember those peanut butter squares I tried on you guys?" Janet chuckles. "We had to eat them with a spoon."

"Remember the popcorn I made, when I forgot to put the lid on the pot?" Paul asks.

I scan their faces as they share memories I'm not part of, and I feel left out.

After a while, Dad says, "Time to get back to work," and picks up the glasses to return them to the kitchen. "We still have lots of unpacking to do. Cassie, do you want to give me a hand?"

I'm about to say, "Sure, Dad," when Janet cries, "Oh, no, James, please! I can't do a thing with Sabina around, and you said Cassie's good with babies. Could she possibly take over for an hour or two?"

"What do you say, Cassie?" Dad asks. "It sure would help."

I swallow my disappointment and say, "Sure, okay."

Paul plunks the baby in my arms and takes off after Dad. Janet thanks me, kisses the baby, and says, "You're a good sport, Cassie. I'll be in the kitchen if you need me."

Sabina leans away from me, watching her mother disappear. She starts to **whimper**, and her eyes fill with doubt and fear. *Why should I trust you?* she seems to be wondering. Then her little mouth curls, and she's crying.

"Come on now, Bina," I whisper, jiggling her up and down, "don't cry. We'll have fun. It's okay, I'm your sister!" I jiggle her some more and sing "Twinkle, Twinkle" and "Old MacDonald," but she doesn't care—she just cries like her little heart is broken.

I carry her into the house, looking for help, but Janet's on a ladder lining shelves, Dad's fixing a towel rack, and Paul's in the garage, bringing in more boxes to unpack.

I take her to the room we share and lie on the bed with my arms wrapped around her delicate **frame**. Her legs feel so new and soft, and she smells so sweet, like sunshine. I make up a song about me and her and our best friend, Eeyore. Soon she forgets I'm a stranger and pulls at Eeyore's nose and tail and tastes his ragged ear. "Ah ga," she says with her head tipped sideways, and I have to laugh.

That's when Paul comes in and announces that Janet wants me to help him pick lemons. *Why does it take two people to pick a couple of lemons?* I think to myself.

I deliver Sabina to Janet and go out to the yard, and wouldn't you know—Paul hides in the tree and throws a lemon at me! He's fifteen years old, going on ten!

"James is going to build a treehouse for Sabina," he says. Boy, that hurts! "And Dad's buying me a car for my birthday."

*Dad?* How dare he call *my father* "Dad," like they're close or something? I can't **tolerate** one more second with him and run into the house.

By dinnertime, he won't even look at me. He's angry that Janet and I are getting along. We were laughing in the kitchen when he came in. Janet was telling me about her first kiss and how she couldn't figure out how to position her nose so it wouldn't get in the way. Paul wanted to know what was so funny, but she wouldn't say.

At dinner he's mad at Dad for bringing up the girlfriend he had to leave behind, for asking me to offer advice about making new friends, and for ruining his **macho** image. He storms off to his room, and I roll my eyes, thinking, *What a baby!* It's nice with him gone.

Dad tells Janet about some of the fun things we used to do, and Janet tells me how she first met Dad when she lent him a quarter for a parking meter and he tracked her down to pay it back. As we're cleaning up the pizza mess, Janet says, "Paul's in a **sulk**. His male ego's been hurt. You know how guys are—they think they can solve the world's problems."

Dad clears his throat, and I suspect Janet's talking about him, too.

"Anyway," Janet says, "I hate for him to feel left out. I could go talk to him, or James could, but maybe if you went..."

"Let him be," Dad says. "He'll get over it."

"It's hard on him, too, James," Janet says.

"I'll go," I say, wanting to please Janet. I go to Paul's room and knock, but I don't know what I'll say—I only know how he must feel. He doesn't want to talk to me, of course, but when I apologize for causing trouble between him, his mom, and my dad, he's suddenly listening.

I think, without saying, how I didn't want to come for the weekend because I wouldn't belong. Well, I don't yet, but I see the possibility. I want to say, "Paul, you already belong—let me, too," but instead I say, "I've got to get along with all of you if I want to spend time with my dad. That's all I came to say."

Something in his face changes even as I turn away. He grabs my arm, and suddenly he's nice—he invites me into his room, puts on a CD, and questions me about the high school he'll be going to.

And all of a sudden—I don't know why or how—we're talking.


## Paul

Oh, man, what a baby! There she stands in the doorway—Cassie, my stepsister, visiting for the first time for a weekend and looking like she's just been shown into the dentist's office to have all her teeth pulled. I'm in total disbelief—she's 13 years old, and she's still hugging a stuffed animal!

"I expect you to be nice to her," Mom had said earlier. "She's James's daughter and it's got to be hard on her, coming here, especially when we're so busy settling into our new home."

"Poor baby," I said.

"Stop that," Mom cried, giving me a nasty look. "Your stepfather has been very good to you, Paul, and you'll show your appreciation by helping Cassie feel comfortable!"

So, okay, I give it a shot. I join the greeting party at the door, I play **porter** and bring her bag to her room, and then, just to test the water, I make a joke about the donkey she hangs onto for dear life. Instantly, out come the fangs, and I'm out of there like a light!

Fifteen minutes later, James has unglued her from that thing she carries and **lured** her outside. We've got home-baked cookies in her honor, we've put a cloth on the picnic table, and we've taken time out from all the work we've got to do. But is she into it? No way!

She watches Mom like maybe she's a killer, eyes James like a starving person **peering** into a bakery window, and refuses to make eye contact with me at all. When it's time to get back to work, Mom asks if Cassie can watch Sabina, and I see the mental wheels spinning: *Is that why I'm here—to be a baby-sitter all weekend?*

I get a special kick out of putting Sabina in her arms. Who knows, a couple of hours with Bina and maybe she won't visit again—which wouldn't break my heart. Who needs a girl to share the bathroom with? Besides, my stepdad and I get along pretty well now. Who needs the competition?

"Bring me some lemons from the tree out back, Paul," Mom says a while later, "and take Cassie along with you."

"All right," I say and trot off to the baby's room. The door's partly open and I hear Cass singing, so I walk right in. Sabina's sitting on my stepsister's lap, happily chewing on that old stuffed donkey with its 13 years of germs.

Cassie looks up, and for a second she's got the same sweet expression Sabina gets sometimes, but then she sees me, and her eyes turn dark and distant.

"Mom says it's time for Sabina's dinner," I

say. "She wants us to pick some lemons. Why don't you meet me out back?" Then I turn around before she has a chance to whip out her fangs again.

The lemon tree is old, like the house, and most of the lemons are rotting on the ground. I climb up on a limb to reach some of the better ones and see Cass heading across the lawn.

"Paul, Paul," she calls, looking for me.

"Catch," I shout, tossing a lemon in her direction. It almost hits her, and she jumps, startled, which isn't what I expected to happen.

We sit on opposite limbs, kind of looking and not looking at each other. I pick a lemon and hold it to my nose, while she swings her legs and checks out the view.

"I'm sorry I screamed at you before," she says.

"I'm sorry I teased you," I say.

She plucks a lemon, smells it, and takes a bite without **flinching**. I'm thinking she's not such a bad kid after all if she has the guts to apologize.

"We had a house, too," she says, **wistfully**,

"and we had two dogs and a cat, a swimming pool, and 20 rose bushes." She brightens when she adds, "Dad taught me to play tennis, and when I was younger, he built me a treehouse!"

"James says he'll build a treehouse for Sabina when she's big enough," I say. My words seem to wound her, though I don't intend them to, and—to make matters worse—I add, "Dad's buying me a car for my birthday!"

"Your dad's buying you a car?"

"No, Dad—you know, James!"

There's fire in her eyes when she says, "He's

not your dad! Don't call him that! You have a father—Dad is mine!"

"Psssssh!"

She bites her lip and turns away. "Shouldn't we be picking lemons?" She plucks two, then drops to the ground with a thud and heads into the house.

I almost feel sorry for her, until I think, *why?* She's a snake—if I'm nice to her, she'll only want to hang around me whenever she visits.

Mom sends me off to the store, and when I walk into the kitchen later with the pizza for dinner, Cassie's at the sink, washing salad stuff and giggling. "What's so funny?" I ask. Mom exchanges knowing glances with Cass and says, "Girl talk." There's silence until I leave, then the giggling starts again. I don't like it—this is my house, my mom!

"Paul's worried about going to a new high school," James says at dinner. "It's hard for him, leaving all his old friends—even a girlfriend— right, pal?" James winks at me.

I feel like he's punched me in the gut,

reminding me about Tina and school, making me look weak in front of my stepsister. "Hey, James, I'm *not* worried," I say.

Cassie eyes me with interest. "When we moved after the divorce, I had to go to another school, too, and it was hard to fit in at first."

"Do you have any suggestions to make it easier for Paul?" Mom asks.

That's it—I can't take it anymore. "Hey, cut it out, all of you! I can manage my own life," I cry.

"No one said you couldn't, Paul, but if Cassie can help—" Mom says.

"Oh, sure, some help she'd be! She'd probably say, 'Take your teddy bear along!'"

I'm in big trouble now. Mom's voice drops to an angry low: "Apologize to Cass this minute, Paul! Apologize or go to your room!"

"Oh, no, it's okay," Cass **interjects**, trying to smooth things over, but I'm already up and out of there like a rocket.

I lie on my bed with my hands under my head, staring at a spot on the ceiling. I hear their voices in the other room, James's deep one, Mom's high-pitched one, Cassie's. They're talking and laughing—they don't even notice I'm gone! She's only been here a few hours, and already she's moving in on my family—my mom, my stepdad, even my baby sister!

"Paul?" It's Cassie at the door, knocking. I'd have thought James might come or Mom, but not her.

"Go away," I tell her.

"Can I talk to you for a second?" she asks.

"Go away!"

"Not till you let me apologize."

*Why would* she *want to apologize?* Curious, I go to the door and open it.

"What do you want?" I ask, but I block the door so she can't come in.

"I just want to say I'm sorry," she says. "I seem to be saying that a lot here. I didn't mean to cause trouble between you and your mom and my dad."

"Yeah, well..." I'm thrown off balance. "I guess I shouldn't have said what I did. It's not easy for you either."

"No," she agrees, looking beyond me. I can see she'd like to come in, but I stand my ground.

"Janet's nice. I didn't want to like her, but I do. You're really lucky. I really miss Dad. I guess I've got to get along with all of you if I want to have any time with him." She turns away. "That's all I wanted to say."

I get a knot in my stomach, like the way I feel when I have to spend a day with my father. It's hard to reconnect. Usually, I haven't seen him in a while, and, usually, I have to share him with some lady friend and her kids. That's how it must be for Cass. Poor kid, she's smarter and more mature than I thought.

"Hey, Cassie, wait," I say, grabbing her arm and pulling her back. Maybe we *can* be friends.

"What?" She resists me, not quite sure what I'm up to.

"Come in my room for a minute—I bought a new CD yesterday." I lead her into my room and go right to my stereo. Casually, as if it doesn't really matter, I ask, "You know much about Lincoln High?"

"A little," she says, sitting on the floor with her back against my bed.

"What's it like? How did you make new friends?"

"Well," she says—and suddenly she's talking like we've known each other all our lives.

And I'm listening.

# Calling Jack Kettle

Norma Fox Mazer

Meadow wanted to call Jack Kettle—that is, she wanted Jessie to call him, but not say who she was or who she was calling for. Meadow had noticed Jack behind the counter at the Clubhouse one day, and she hadn't stopped talking about him since—how good-looking he was, what a sweet smile he had, what a great build.

"Etcetera, etcetera," Jessie broke in. They were upstairs in Meadow's room. "I'm past the stage of making **anonymous** calls to boys, Med, and you should be, too."

"Jessie," Meadow's pale little face flamed, "you know how I am."

"Shy," Jessie sighed.

"*Massively* shy," Meadow exclaimed.

"What if you just strike up a conversation with him at the Clubhouse?" Jessie asked.

"Do *what*?" Meadow sounded shocked by the very suggestion.

"Then what if I make the call, but you talk to him?"

"Jessie—"

"What if I get things started and then hand you the phone?" She didn't even wait for Meadow's protest, she just dialed Jack's number. Why not—she'd been speaking for Meadow ever since they became best friends, way back in kindergarten.

"Hello," said a voice on the other line.

"Jack Kettle, please," Jessie said.

"Speaking," he replied.

"Ahh, Jack," Jessie cleared her throat and lowered her voice to what she hoped was a low, fascinating **drawl**, "how fortunate that I found you in. I have a message for you: Someone I know thinks you are *very* interesting."

"You mean you?" Jack asked.

"If I meant myself, Jack, I would say so."

He laughed. "You sound cute."

Meadow was breathing warmly on Jessie's neck. "Jack," Jessie said, "believe me, I'm not your type."

"So this other girl, is she pretty?"

"Is that all that matters to you guys? However, if you must know, yes, she's pretty— blonde, with big brown eyes, plus she's smart and athletic, and she has an adorable mole near her mouth."

"Ssss," Meadow hissed, digging her chin warningly into Jessie's shoulder. "She's blonde?" Jack asked, clearly **intrigued**.

Jessie sighed—didn't he hear anything else she'd said? "Tell me, Jack, why do you boys always get excited about blondes?"

He laughed again. "I don't know. What's her name?"

"Now, now, Jack, that's a secret, but I'll give you a hint: Her first initial is M."

"Marylee Farber?" he asked, his voice rising slightly.

"Don't you wish," Jessie replied. Marylee was a senior who had been elected prom queen last year and was a shoo-in for **valedictorian** this year.

"Melody Farmer?"

"No, Jack."

"Misty Alzicia, Margaret—"

"Wrong, wrong, wrong again. Bye, bye, Jack, no more guesses for you."

Jessie put down the phone.

"You told him about my mole," Meadow complained, touching the corner of her mouth. "He's going to know who I am."

"Is that the thanks I get for doing your dog work?" Jessie demanded.

"What do you want me to do?" Meadow asked.

"Grovel at my feet, say I'm a wonderful friend...."

"You're a wonderful friend."

"I know," Jessie said, smiling modestly.

The next time they called Jack Kettle, they were in Jessie's house. A woman answered the phone. "Could I speak to Jack, please?" Jessie asked.

"Who's calling?"

"Aaah, just tell him it's a friend," Jessie said **vaguely**.

"Just a moment—Jack!"

"Jessie, was that his mother?" Meadow whispered.

"I think so, Meadow."

"How did she sound?"

"Like a mother, Meadow."

"Hello," Jack said.

"Jack, this is your mystery friend, speaking on behalf of MBC, or should I say the *fabulous* MBC," Jessie said.

"Is that for Most Beautiful Creature?"

"Very good, Jack!"

"What school do you go to?" Jack asked.

"That's for me to know and you to wonder, Jack. You know nothing about me, and that's the way it should be. I, however, sort of know what you look like, where you work, and—"

"You're giving him too many clues," Meadow whispered urgently.

"When am I going to meet you in person?" he said. "You sound so cute, and your voice— you have a great voice!"

"Did you ever hear a bad voice, Jack? Don't bother answering that. I'm not cute. And now you're thinking, *If she's not cute, why am I talking to her?*"

"I'm not thinking that," Jack cried.

"Sure you are," Jessie replied. "Goodbye, Jack. I'm tired of talking to you."

"Why did you hang up on him, Jessie?" Meadow whispered.

"Because I felt like it, Meadow. He was boring me. Why are we whispering?"

The third call to Jack Kettle was from a phone booth in front of a gas station on Nottingham Road. "I wouldn't do this for anyone but you," Jessie said.

"I know," Meadow replied, setting her guitar case down.

"Prepare for disappointment," Jessie added instructively. "He was home the first two times, so there's no way he'll be home this time—it's the law of averages, Meadow."

Jack Kettle answered on the first ring.

"*Law of averages, Meadow,*" Meadow mouthed **tauntingly** at Jessie.

"Hey, it's the girl with the voice," Jack Kettle said.

"Hey, it's the boy with the laugh."

He laughed.

"Did you ever think, Jack, that our planet is like a huge **sprawling** house, and we humans are like the family that moved in and forgot to pay the rent?"

"Huh?"

"When the family moved in, they thought they had more rooms than they'd ever need, so they didn't bother cleaning up their messes. If a room got too gross, they just shut the door and trekked on to a nice fresh room."

"Jessie, what are you doing?" Meadow hissed.

But Jessie continued, "A long time passed, Jack, and they started having trouble with the house. The plumbing wasn't the greatest anymore, the roof was leaking, and nearly every room was in use." She paused. "What do you think about all this, Jack?"

"He doesn't think anything," Meadow said. "He's gone." She had her finger pressed down on the switch. "You were boring him, Jessie." She picked up her guitar case and walked away.

"How do you know that?" Jessie said, going after her.

"Because you were boring me! Besides, there wasn't anything about *me* in that conversation."

"Meadow, I can't mention your name, I can't say how you look, I can't say that you know him from the Clubhouse. What am

I supposed to say?"

"I don't know," Meadow said.

"Besides, he's a muscle-bound jerk. Why don't you get a crush on someone who's smart?"

"He's not a jerk," Meadow protested.

"All those guys with muscles are jerks."

"You make me so mad when you say stupid things like that!"

"And you make me mad when you say the things I say are stupid!"

They glared at each other for a moment. Then Meadow went one way, toward her guitar lesson, and Jessie went the other, toward the diner where her mother worked.

In the morning, Jessie was in a bad mood, as she was whenever she and Meadow **quarreled**. The worst part about it this time was that today was the annual Save the County Walk. This was the third year Jessie had signed up, and, grumpy as she felt, she still wasn't going to miss it. Her mother drove her to the park where the walk started.

Her team consisted of an older man with big square teeth, a couple wearing identical denim outfits, and a boy in baggy striped pants and a camouflage hat pulled down over his eyes.

Jessie started filling up her garbage bag, darting at every glimmer of glass and metal. There was something **gratifying** about doing this—it was the same feeling she had when she attacked her room after a long period of grunge.

The older people had drifted to the other side of the road, where they were laughing and having a good time, while she and the boy hadn't said a word. After what seemed like five hundred minutes of silence, Jessie said to him, "I heard there are a couple hundred people on this walk."

"Uh huh," he replied.

*Just my luck to be stuck with a brilliant* **conversationalist**, she thought, stooping to pick up a slimy piece of plastic. "Two hundred out of the quarter of a million residents—you'd think a few more would want to save it."

He glanced at her and dipped into the flattened grass for some beer cans.

"This is my third year doing this," she said, trying to start a conversation again.

"Yeah?"

"And it always rains," she continued. "It's a law—even though the sun is shining when the walk begins, it has to rain before it's over."

He laughed. *Well, that was an improvement,* she thought.

"How about you?" she inquired. "How many years have you been going on this walk?"

"This is my first time," he said.

"Congratulations." *For saying five words,* she thought to herself.

She felt his eyes on her as she rolled a tire toward the road and tagged it for the truck.

"Eight ten-thousandths of a percent," he said suddenly.

"What?"

"Two hundred people is eight ten-thousandths of one percent of a quarter of a million."

"You calculated that in your head?" Jessie asked.

He blushed. "I'm going to study **sanitary engineering**—math is useful."

She bent down to clean up some broken glass, and he knelt down, too, putting them nose to nose. Suddenly he said, "Those are some eyebrows you have!"

"Well, they're mine," Jessie said, a little defensively.

"I didn't say I didn't like them," he replied.

They walked again, and this time he started the conversation. "I have an idea that the earth is like a big house with lots of rooms, and humans are the family who live in the house."

Jessie stared at him, speechless for once.

"Do you realize we're using up all the clean rooms?" he asked.

"I think I do," she managed. She'd realized something else, too, though she was surprised she hadn't figured it out sooner. "That's a great idea, Jack," she said.

He actually jumped with surprise. "You know my name?"

"I guess I do." *Oh, why torture him?* "You work at the Clubhouse, don't you?"

"Did you see me working out on the machines?" he asked hopefully.

Jessie raised one of the eyebrows that **awed** him. "Oh, man, watching guys work out is not one of my preferred pastimes."

"You're so cute. What's your name?" Jack asked.

"Jessie. Quick, what's yours? Never mind— just testing." She closed the full garbage bag with a twist-tie and left it by the side of the road for the truck. "How did you come up with that idea about the earth being a house?"

"Ahhhh, it's actually not my idea," he admitted, blushing again. "It's my, ahhh, girlfriend's—that is, ah, this girl I talk to on the phone...."

Jessie snapped open a fresh plastic bag, and just then the truth was revealed to her. Jack Kettle was not just a bunch of bulging muscles. Well, he was, but he was more than that. He was also sweet, honest when put to the test, and shy—definitely shy.

Oh, no, not another shy person in her life.

"Bad," Jessie mumbled to herself, "bad, very bad!" She had not only fallen for Meadow's crush but agreed to meet him in the mall on Monday afternoon. When Meadow found out, she was going to die of heartbreak, and then she was going to kill Jessie.

"Two girls, one boy," Jessie wrote in her notebook, "Jessie, Meadow, Jack." Then she perked up for a moment, noticing that she and Jack shared the same first initial. But Meadow had seen him first. Jessie hadn't even liked him, so sure that all his brains had oozed out of his head and into his puffy muscular arms.

*Two girls, one boy, one big mouth*, she thought gloomily. She flung herself down on her bed and considered her options—she could tell Meadow about Jack, or she could *not* tell Meadow about Jack.

*You have to tell her. Bring her to the mall to meet him. Friendship is stronger than a crush.*

That was a noble thought.

Jack would see Meadow and blush—she was so pretty. His face would turn that adorable shade of bright pink, and Meadow would gasp and disappear behind Jessie.

Then what—neither one would say a word. Jessie could see Meadow's face doing a dance of **indecision** as Jack struggled painfully for words.

*Two shy people—that would never work. So don't tell her. Meet him at the mall, and have Jack all to yourself.*

That was a mean, selfish thought.

She held her head in her hands. It was all up to her—she could make things happen any way she wanted them to.

Two girls, one boy. Two crushes, one friendship.

She **staggered** to her feet and stared at herself in the mirror for a long time, pondering what she saw. She saw a girl with a best friend, she saw a girl with a big crush, and she saw a girl who didn't want to give up either one.

**Listlessly**, she took her lip gloss and drew a house with two windows and, in each window, a girl. She made their hands touch. Then, with a little more energy, she drew a boy floating in space outside the house. She added some stars and the sun and the moon, too, while she was at it. She hoped lip gloss wasn't too hard to get off glass. Then she drew a heart around the boy. The girls were smiling as they gazed at him affectionately, and the boy was smiling, too.

She stood back and studied her work of art. What else did it need? She considered making the boy into a heart balloon and giving each one of the girls a string to it, but, finally, she did nothing. The picture was fine just the way it was—two girls, one boy.

# Glossary

**abandoned** *(verb)* gave up; left behind

**affirmative** *(adjective)* expressing agreement or support *(related word: affirm)*

**anonymous** *(adjective)* done by someone whose name is not known

**atmosphere** *(noun)* the mood or feeling

**attributed** *(verb)* gave credit to

**autopsy** *(noun)* the inspection of a dead body to figure out the cause of death

**awed** *(verb)* made a strong impression or had a serious effect on

**ballad** *(noun)* a song or poem that tells a story

*bodega* *(noun)* a small grocery store

**catharsis** *(noun)* a release of emotions, especially through a work of art

**circulating** *(verb)* moving from place to place or person to person

**confided** *(verb)* opened up to someone; told someone a secret

**conversationalist** *(noun)* someone who is good at talking to people *(related word: conversation)*

**corridor** *(noun)* a hallway

**criticisms** *(noun)* judgements or comments made about someone or something *(related word: criticize)*

**declarations** *(noun)* announcements or statements *(related word: declare)*

**desperation** *(noun)* a feeling of hopelessness *(related word: desperate)*

**devastated** *(adjective)* very badly damaged or destroyed; shocked or upset

**diplomatic** *(adjective)* good at dealing with people

**drawl** *(noun)* a way of speaking in which words are drawn out or spoken slowly

**famine** *(noun)* a serious lack of food that affects a large group of people

**feeble** *(adjective)* weak

**flinching** *(verb)* drawing back or tensing up, usually because you're afraid or in pain

**frame** *(noun)* a body

**gnawed** *(verb)* chewed on

**gratifying** *(adjective)* satisfying; pleasurable

**haze** *(noun)* a fog or mist; a confused state of mind

**husky** *(adjective)* rough or hoarse

**indecision** *(noun)* not being able to decide

**inherited** *(verb)* received some talent or characteristic from your parents

**interjects** *(verb)* interrupts; steps in to make a comment

**intrigued** *(adjective)* interested; fascinated

**listlessly** *(adverb)* with little interest or energy; in an absentminded way

**lured** *(verb)* attracted or led a person or creature *(related word: lure)*

**lurking** *(verb)* sneaking around; spying

**macho** *(adjective)* tough or strong; manly

**magnanimously** *(adverb)* in a courageous or confident way

**meter** *(noun)* the rhythm of a line of poetry created by the way the words sound when spoken

**mortar** *(noun)* a type of cement

**mortified** *(adjective)* extremely embarrassed

**nestled** *(adjective)* lying comfortably

**nobler** *(adjective)* more honorable; stronger as a person *(related word: noble)*

**peering** *(verb)* looking carefully or closely

**ploy** *(noun)* a strategy or trick

**pondered** *(verb)* thought about carefully

**porter** *(noun)* someone who is hired to carry packages or bags

**quarreled** *(verb)* argued; fought

**raucous** *(adjective)* rowdy; harsh or rough

**razed** *(verb)* tore down

**registered** *(verb)* showed or indicated

**rigid** *(adjective)* stiff; firm

**riveting** *(adjective)* very interesting

**sanitary engineering** *(noun)* the study of systems that protect the health of people and the environment, for example, a city's water system or sewage system

**sprawling** *(adjective)* spreading out in all different directions

**staggered** *(verb)* moved in an unsteady way

**stanza** *(noun)* a group of lines in a poem

**sulk** *(noun)* a bad mood

**surveillance** *(noun)* the careful watching of someone or something

**tauntingly** *(adverb)* in a teasing or insulting way

**tawdry** *(adjective)* cheap, flashy, tasteless

**tolerate** *(verb)* to put up with

**undercuts** *(verb)* weakens or destroys

**vaguely** *(adverb)* in a way that is not clear or definite

**valedictorian** *(noun)* the student who gives the farewell speech, or valedictory, at graduation. The valedictorian is usually the student with the best grades in the class.

**violate** *(verb)* to disturb rudely or without any right

**whimper** *(verb)* to make weak crying noises

**wistfully** *(adverb)* in a longing or wishful way